Originally published by Country Life in 1939

First published in the United States by Macmillan, New York, in 1967

First Candlewick Press edition 2001

Library of Congress Cataloging-in-Publication Data

Peake, Mervyn Laurence, 1911–1968.
Captain Slaughterboard drops anchor / story and drawings by Mervyn Peake. —2nd U.S. ed.
p.   cm.
Summary: On a fantastic island populated by unusual animals, a pirate captain
finds a trustworthy companion in the little "Yellow Creature."
ISBN 0-7636-1625-7
[1. Pirates—Fiction.] I. Title.
PZ7.P3135 Cap 2001
[Fic]—dc21   2001029510

2 4 6 8 10 9 7 5 3 1

Printed in Italy

This book was lettered and drawn in ink on board.
For this edition, color tinting was designed
by Julia Thompson with assistance from Daniel Devlin.

Candlewick Press
2067 Massachusetts Avenue
Cambridge, Massachusetts 02140

visit us at www.candlewick.com

CANDLEWICK PRESS
CAMBRIDGE, MASSACHUSETTS

CAPTAIN
SLAUGHTERBOARD
DROPS
ANCHOR

STORY ☆ AND
DRAWINGS ☆ BY

MERVYN ☆ PEAKE ☆

Far beyond the jungles and the burning deserts lay the bright blue ocean that stretched for ever in all directions. There were little green islands with undiscovered edges, and whales swam around them in this sort of way.

But the most exciting thing was
the Pirate Ship.
Her name was the Black Tiger
and

Captain Slaughterboard ruled her - every inch!

He looked
like this...

Lots of his men had been eaten by sharks
or killed in battle, and hundreds had been
made to walk the plank.

Here are the ones who were left.

and
Jonas Joints, the first mate, could do this!

Timothy Twitch was the most elegant in battle,
his left hand especially,

and Charlie Choke was covered all over with
dreadful drawings in blue
ink.

Peter Poop was
the cook and

he had a cork nose.

Here is Captain Slaughterboard again, this time pretending to be asleep.
One afternoon while they were sailing over the warm waves they came across a new island.
"Captain," shouted Charlie Choke, "there's some land on the horizon."
"What colour is it?" said Captain Slaughter-board, opening one eye.

"Looks kind of pink to me," said Charlie Choke after a very long time (he wasn't much good at colours).
"Pink!" shouted the Captain, leaping to his feet. "That's just the sort I like. Sail me there and hurry up or I'll chop you all up into mincemeat."

DON'T DISTURB ME UNLESS ITS IMPORTANT YOU DOGS!! Slaughterboard

Then he took out his telescope and

this is what he
saw.

"Rattle my ribs!" he yelled. "There are some preposterous creatures over there! Faster, faster! Sail the ship faster! I must catch one of them before it gets too dark."

When they were quite near the island they all jumped
into a rowing boat and pulled hard
for the shore.

Captain Slaughterboard sat at the back and smoked a huge pipe. He didn't row, of course, but waved his heavy old cutlass about.

"Faster, faster!" he thundered. "Have your muscles fallen off?"

When the sea looked shallow enough they all jumped out of the boat with a great splash, but the water came up to their necks and it felt like a nice warm bath. But the Captain didn't like having baths, and Billy Bottle trod on a crimson jelly-fish with a horrible squelch.

But they had soon waded to the shore.

"Where are the queer creatures?" cried Captain Slaughterboard. "Hurry up and find them, and don't forget what I said about cutting you all up into little pieces!" This made them rather nervous and they ran here and there all over the wet sand and up the palm trees.

Suddenly they heard a husky voice. "Ship ahoy! Captain! Fetch up alongside. I've sighted one!" It was Billy Bottle shouting from the jungle and they all ran towards him. Sure enough, not very far away in the green shadows was a creature as bright as butter.

"Just exactly the sort I've been wanting," yelled Captain Slaughterboard as he charged over the fruit and turtles that covered the ground. "After him, you dogs!"

Billy Bottle was the swiftest because of his long arms, and he caught the Yellow Creature just as it was about to hide in a hollow tree. "Fetch him aboard the Black Tiger," said the Captain, when he had stopped panting. "Careful ... careful ..."

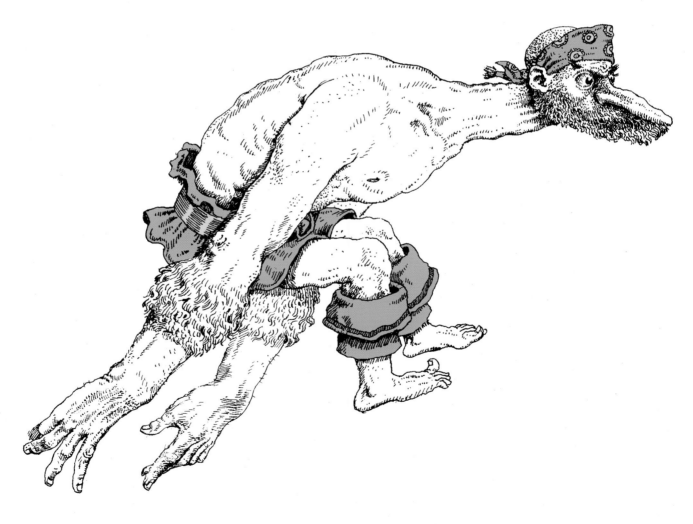

Peter Poop and Jonas Joints walked on each side of the little Yellow Creature, holding its hands.

But the Yellow Creature didn't really want to escape because he had been rather lonely on the island.

You see, nearly all the other creatures were purple.

There was the
Balleroon with
his backbone
made out of
three-ply (that
means very
thin wood)...

And the Dignipomp...

The Lonely Mousterashe who was sensitive and didn't make friends very easily...

And the Hunchabil whose dreadful croaking always got on the Yellow Creature's nerves...

And the Guggaflop who was very, very lazy...

And the
Saggerdroop
with his
melancholy
eyes
as rich
as topaz ...

Not to speak
of the two
loathsome
Squirmarins.

They all hid in the shadows of the warm rocks and watched the Pirates take the Yellow Creature away in a rowing boat.

All except the Sleeka and his son who watched it all happening with their heads sticking out of the smooth sea...

And the Plummet who lived in a deep world under the waves, among the starfish and the sponges, the fishes and the pearls.

He couldn't *see* that anything was happening but he *felt* it was.

Soon they were on
board again and
the Captain gave
the Yellow Creature
a cabin to himself,
and was furious when
Timothy Twitch
pulled his ears for
fun. The Pirates
were very puzzled
and couldn't
understand it at all
because Captain
Slaughterboard was
a wicked sort of man
and had never been pleasant
to strangers before.

Poor Timothy didn't know what to think.

Every morning the Yellow Creature was placed in the front of the ship, where he looked lovely against the sparkling blue sea. Captain Slaughterboard would sit upon a barrel of rum, and watch the Yellow Creature for hours on end.

His Pirates had to watch the Yellow Creature too, but they got rather tired of it sometimes...

Every thirty
minutes Peter
Poop was made
to take the
Yellow Creature
a tray of nice
things to eat.
If he was

late with it the Captain ground his teeth
in a horrible way and made his sword sing
through the hot air.

One starry night, at
twenty-three minutes
past twelve, Captain
Slaughterboard felt a
bit bored, so he heaved
up the anchor with one
jerk, and

they sailed away and right over the
horizon where they met with so many
adventures and such terrible battles
that at last the Yellow Creature and
the Captain were the only ones left on board. They always had
their meals together.

Captain Slaughterboard
taught the Yellow Creature
some old pirate dances
and they would practise
them together when the
moon was full.

One evening as they leaned upon the railing and threw some plums and peaches to a dark speckly fish...

"Yellow Creature," said Captain Slaughterboard.

"Yo-ho," said the Yellow Creature (it was the only expression that he had learned from the crew).

"I feel a bit tired of battles and things," said the Captain. The Yellow Creature looked up sympathetically.

"Yo-ho," he said again. Captain Slaughterboard walked up and down the sloping deck seven times with great strides.

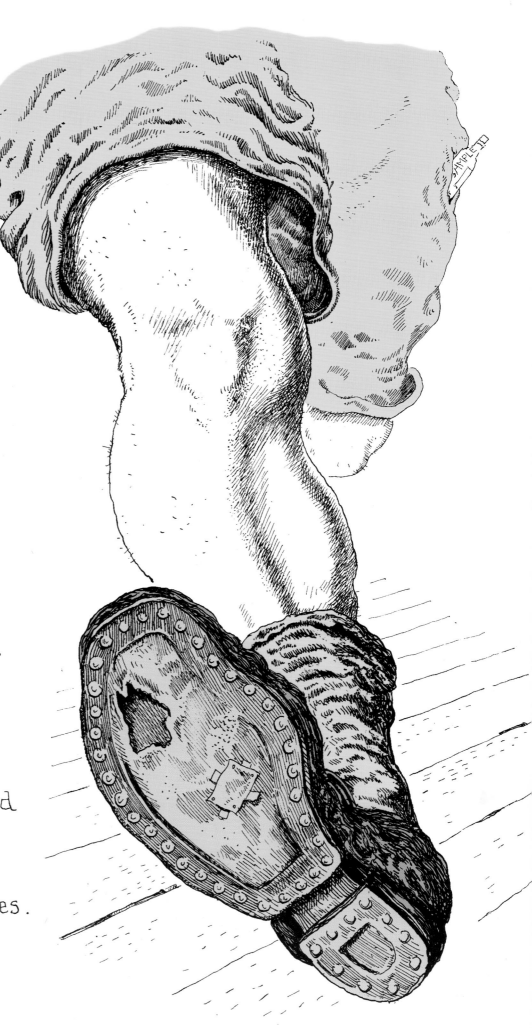

"We'll sail back to that island and explore the jungles and climb to the tops of the mountains," he said. The Yellow Creature must have understood for he got very excited and danced around in a wild sort of way shouting "Yo-ho! Yo-ho! Yo-ho!"

So they turned the ship around and sailed as fast as they could back to the island. Captain Slaughterboard did the steering and the Yellow Creature saw to the sails.

Lots of whales got in the way but they dodged them all, and one beautiful bright morning they saw on the horizon a little pink speck. It was the island again.

They dropped
anchor in the
clear water
when they
were near to the
shore. The Cap-
tain lowered the
Yellow Creature,
his gun, and
some bottles of
rum into the
rowing boat
and pulled for
the beach.
The island
looked so fresh
and bright
with the trees
so green, and
the sand so
yellow, as
though every-
thing had just been painted, with a big blue mountain sticking up
in the middle like a great claw.

When they had dragged the little boat over the shingle and onto the hot sand, the Yellow Creature showed Captain Slaughterboard all the exciting parts of the island...

The waterfalls and the lagoons, the caves in the blue mountain and the secret tracks through the jungle.

They met the Guggaflop, who
was practically asleep as usual
but who grunted quite politely
when they said "How do you do?"
Soon they had met most of the
inhabitants, who were really very
friendly.

After a week or two Captain Slaughterboard began to wish that he could live there all his life.

Suddenly one morning he said to himself, "Well, why shouldn't I?"

He was the only
one left out of all
his Pirates after
all, so why should
he go sailing around and searching for battles
all by himself?   "Ahoy! Yellow Creature!"
he called. "I'm staying here for good!" The
Yellow Creature, who was frantic with joy, shouted "Yo-ho" fifty times.

They are still on the island. The Captain would never dream of leaving and can't understand how he used to enjoy killing people so much. The Yellow Creature does the cooking and can make the most exciting things to eat out of practically nothing.

Captain
Slaughterboard finished
up all his bullets long
ago, but they have both
become very good with
bows and arrows, and

can hit things a long
way off.

But most of the time they are dreadfully lazy and
eat fruit.

Or lie
upon the
rocks in
the sun,

and catch
strange
glittering
fishes...

Like this,

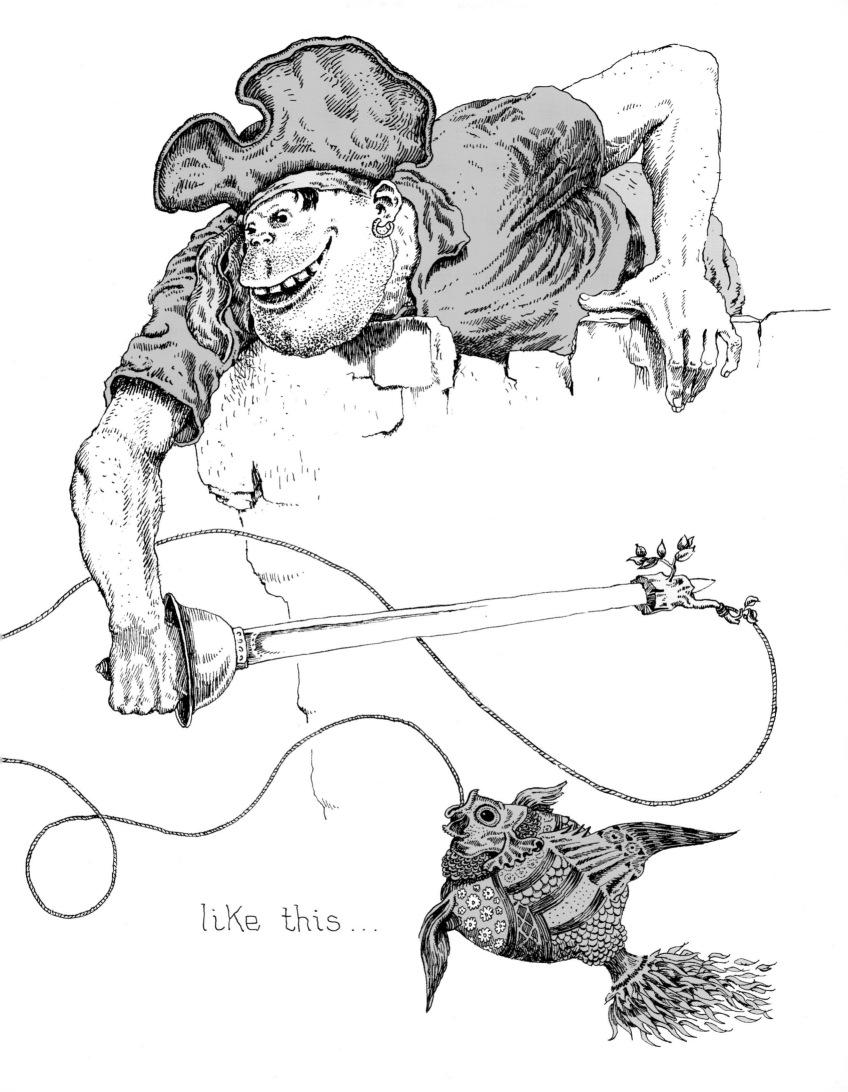

like this...

Or
liKe
this.

A Word About This Book
Fabian Peake

As a young man in the 1930s, my father, Mervyn Peake, visited Sark, one of the Channel Islands, with the idea of living a bohemian life free from the pressures of modern society. Soon after the Second World War, he returned with his wife, Maeve, and their two sons, Sebastian and myself, Fabian. A daughter, Clare, was born on the island in 1949. At the time, Sark was an isolated place, and living conditions were simple. Water had to be hand pumped; lighting was by means of paraffin lamps; and apart from tractors, no motorized vehicles were allowed on the island. Our parents had provided us with an idyllic early childhood, and we were swept along in the wash of my father's colossal spirit of adventure.

Each Sunday in his study, a large room with an open fire, my father would make drawings for my brother and me. Typically, these were of pirates, comical animals, and monstrous scenes in pen and ink, watercolor, or pencil, which we collected in special books. These drawings were clearly from the same imagination that created the eccentric characters of *Captain Slaughterboard Drops Anchor*.

In this beautiful new edition, my father's book has been produced as it was intended. No details have been spared, and the idiosyncracies of his original idea have been properly realized.

London, March 2001